GOBBLE, GOBBLE LOOK WHO'S COMING TO THANKSGIVING DINNER.

Karen Ligocki

ISBN: 978-1-965666-89-0

Printed in the United States of America

Chapter 1

Waking up in the hospital Jesse, couldn't focus, his eyes were blurry, was it day or night? His mouth felt like saw dust and the only reason, he knew he was in the hospital, was the awful bed and the smell of cleaners.

"Good Morning Jesse."

"Can you tell me, who I'm talking to? I can't see you, why can't I see anything? Everything is blurry."

"It's Dr Roman, Jesse."

Okay, he knew Kingsley Roman.

They've been friends since Jesse moved to Maine, King was working as a mover to pay for Med school.

"King? King, Why can't I see?"

Dr Roman was happy Jesse recognized him.

"Jess, I'm not sure about your vision, I'm going to have someone check on that. Jesse you being out for 5 days, after your surgery they couldn't wake you up. Maddie's here, I made her, go get something to eat. Your shoulder was destroyed Jesse, the surgeon tried his best to put it back together."

Jesse only heard Maddie was here.

"It burns."

"I'll have Joelle get you some pain Medicine, are you allergic to anything?"

"No, do you remember how long Maddie's been gone?"

"She should be back shortly, try to relax, Jess, I know that's easier said than done."

Maddie ran into the room.

"Oh thank God, nobody told me, you were awake. King, can I.."

"I'd be really gentle"

Maddie went to Jesse and wrapped her arms around him. Jesse groaned. Maddie tried to pull away but Jesse held her tight.

"No, please." He buried his face in her neck. "I love you Maddie, I want to get married, today."

"Today?"

Jesse groaned.

"Today is fine, I have to comb my hair" Jesse tried to laugh, but there was a splitting pain burning his right shoulder.

"Baby, if anything should happen to me.. "

"Don't you dare, Jesse Wiseman, don't you dare finish that sentence. King, tell him."

Maddie looked back at Dr Roman. King looked from his friend to Maddie.

"Maddie, he lost a lot of blood, he is stable but critical, that's the best I can say. I'm sorry."

Maddie looked back at Jesse, he was asleep

Okay.

Maddie was at her wit's end, not even knowing if it was night or day.

I need a shower and real coffee, but I'm not leaving, of course, if they throw me out.

Jesse let out a huge groan, Maddie jumped up, but Jesse never woke up. King said it was really bad that Jesse was experiencing that much pain, while on morphine and asleep.

Maddie was scared to leave Jesse, she didn't care if she sounded crazy. She asked Dorie and Vee to find her a wedding dress and his and her bands.

I'll be damn if something happens and we are not married. The hospital gave permission. Maddie got a priest and some flowers while Paul brought a tux. Hoping Jesse would wake up,

Maddie sat beside him and held his hand. Jesse squeezed her hand. Maddie sat upright.

"Jesse baby, can you hear me?"

Maddie's excitement diminished after 5 minutes, and then ever so slightly Jesse's hand moved, Maddie closed her eyes, sighing.

"Jesse, Jess come back to me."

Just above a whisper, Jesse groaned "Mads"

"Jess, listen to me, I am going to ask you a question, squeeze my hand if your answer is yes."

Jesse's breathing was jerky, probably due to the pain, Maddie waited til it was calmer.

"Jess, we are going to get married tonight, okay? Everything is ready to go, I just wanted to be sure it's what you want." There was no squeeze, no eye flickering. Maddie didn't know if he was asleep or his answer was no, 'Really dumb, Maddie, ' she scolded herself.

"Mads, yes"

"Oh thank Goodness. Jess, listen to me, okay, I need you, Jess, I really need you, we are having a baby."

A deep loud groan came out of Jessie, almost animal-like, his alarms went off, and nurses and doctors ran in.

Maddie got pushed back into the corner. Maddie's eyes met King's.

"Get her, out of here, now."

Joelle grabbed Maddie's arm.

"Come on, honey, let them, do their job."

"What's happening, Jo?

"I'm not sure, Maddie. All I know is Dr. Roman wanted you out. Go get something to eat or drink, I'll have someone come and get you."

Maddie told Joelle, she'd be in the waiting room. Joelle worried about Maddie, she hadn't left the hospital, and she barely ate anything, only focusing on the wedding in the sheriff's really room tonight.. tonight. Jo saw the obvious signs of Maddie's pregnancy, nobody had to tell her, and she could spot a pregnant woman, a mile away.

Another groan came from Jesse's, Maddie's insides curled.

Dr. Roman came down the hallway, looking none too happy.

"Maddie, I'm just going to tell you, like it is. Jesse has some damage axillary artery and brachial plexus, he's going to need surgery on his shoulder, on top of that, it's infected. I'd like to introduce you to the surgical specialist, who will be performing the surgery. Maddie, this is Doctor Shirley Waylon."

Maddie and Doctor Waylon exchanged pleasantries. Maddie needed assurance.

"Is Jesse going to be okay?"

Dr Waylon looked at Maddie,

"Maddie, I am going into this blind, we see an infection, we see the bullet lodged deep into a web of nerves. I want to tell you,

Jesse is going to be fine."

"But you can't can you."

"Your husband is in excellent physical condition, he is going to come out of this great. The damage to his nerves, it's a wait and see, that is the best news, I can give you."

Another scream came from Jesse's room. Maddie had tears running down her face.

"Can't you help him?"

"Maddie, he's on the highest dose of pain medication, I can give him. It's the bullet, we scheduled him for emergency surgery, as soon as an OR opens."

Maddie nodded as she hugged herself tight.

Chapter 2

Walking back to the waiting room, noticed the crowd of people. Her family, the Wiseman's, with all the wedding gear. Maddie sighed. As she walked toward them, Maddie felt lightheaded, her legs dragged. Someone yelled catch her. Who shut out the lights, Maddie thought to herself as she felt herself falling.

Benny caught Maddie before her head hit the floor, he lifted her just as a stretcher got there.

All eyes went to the boy, with the stretcher. Deacon Jr.

Paul grabbed Benny and pushed him against the wall, as Joelle shouted to get Maddie to ER. Deacon grabbed the stretcher and wheeled Maddie away.

Dorie looked at Joelle.

"That boy, he's involved."

"Look, I know all about, his bail was posted, he said he was only there, he didn't do anything. I have my eye on him."

Dorie, the rage in her.

"He was there, he threatened my brother, that guy in there, in agony. HE THREATENED MY BROTHER."

"Please, keep your voice down."

"Deacon tells you, he was just there and you believe him?"

"Yes." Joelle's patience was wearing thin.

Dorie could not believe, what she was hearing. "Why?"

"Deacon is my nephew, he's a good kid, got in with the wrong crowd. Just like his father. I'm sorry, I have patients."

Jesse's screams filled the hospital halls. As Joelle turned away, her shoulders dropped, but she turned back.

"I'll check his pain meds, he might have to be put into a medically induced coma. Again, I'm sorry."

Dorie turned, not knowing what to say. Paul grabbed Dorie, pulling her to him, motioning Benny in too.

Paul looked at his kids.

"Look, promise me both of you, you will take care of yourselves. Maddie, she didn't look good at all."

Dorie hugged her father tighter and pulled her brother closer. Pregnant women, shouldn't be pushing themselves like Maddie was, Dorie didn't say anything,

to her father or Benny, but she saw all the signs.

Dr Roman came down the hallway.

"Hello, I guess I'm giving you updates now. So an OR opened and they are preparing Jesse for surgery. I'm going to let you know because of the situation where that artery is still

healing. "He looked at his friend's family. "A few prayers wouldn't hurt, okay."

King hugged Dorie, he always felt something for Dorie but never acted on it because of his friendship with Jesse. He shook hands with Benny and Paul, nodded, and walked away.

Max passed King in the hall, they exchanged hellos. Getting to the group, Max kissed Dorie,

"Guys." he nodded at them.

Max looked around.

"Where's Mads?"

Dorie put her around Max. It made Max smile and his heart soared.

"The hospital is taking care of her, she passed out."

"What? why?"

"She is probably dehydrated."

Paul laughed.

"Dad?"

Paul looked at his daughter.

"Come on, Dorie, I went through three pregnancies with your mom. Your brother is gonna be a dad."

"Daddy!!! Maddie probably didn't tell him yet. Quiet."

Paul laughed. "Okay, sorry."

Benny looked at his father.

"Aww Benny, I'm sorry, I know how much you want to be a dad"

Paul stroked the back of Benny's head. Benny looked confused.

"Actually, I was wondering, since there's no wedding, if we are still having cake."

Paul and Dorie looked at each other and burst out laughing.

Only Benny, they were remembering when he was about three and over at Paul's brother's house for a birthday party, and while everyone was in the other room. Benny grabbed a spoon, climbed up on the table, and dug into the middle of the cake. When Paul went to find his son, he let out an "Oh Benny" and called out to Jessica. Paul then ran out to get a new bigger cake.

When his brother, realized the cake was different, Paul told everyone what happened.

Everyone started calling Benny, cake boy, and until this day, Benny still loves cake. Dorie couldn't help it. "Cake Boy!!"

Benny turned a sheepish grin.

"I just didn't want it to go to waste." The three of them laughed harder. Max just stood there, trying to figure out this crazy family, and shook his head.

Nope, can't be done.

"What's the word on Jess."

It was like the three Wisemans,

suddenly remembered where they were, and why.

"He's being prepped for more surgery, " Dorie said.

Max just looked at her, he loved Jesse like a brother. "What?"

"The bullet is lodged deep in a nerve, in his shoulder, if I understood King right."

"There has to be more to it than that, I'm sure he's in pain but…"

Dorie cut Max off.

"It hit an artery, he lost a lot of blood, that and the fact it's in a pretty bad place, they are not sure the damage"

Dorie started to cry and Max held her against his chest. Max didn't say everything would be okay, he didn't believe in that, that was to God.

Paul cleared his throat and looked at Benny. "Come on Benny, let's go get a cup of coffee, standing or sitting here isn't going to help us. You two, want something for when we come back?" Max motioned for two coffees and Dorie asked for toast realizing she hadn't eaten all day. My big brother, my idol, my life, dear God, please please let him be okay, Dorie sent up prayers.

It was 2 more hours before Doctor Waylon made her way, down the hallway. She has a poker face on, gosh is she good, her face was unreadable. Dr Waylon looked tired, though, it showed in her shoulders.

Shirley Waylon got to the Wisemans, she gave a little encouraging smile.

"Jesse is stable and resting,

he'll be in recovery for a few hours, after that, we will move him to the ICU. He's going to need a lot of medical attention right now. "

Dorie hugged Doctor Waylon.

"Don't thank me yet, Dori. Jesse is far out of the fire zone, he may have lost the use of his left arm, to the point of it being lame, and he more than likely won't be able to perform his job, anymore."

Jesse's family just looked at Doctor Waylon. That was like saying his life was over, Jesse was a law officer. Being a Sheriff was who he was. That's who he was. Paul spoke.

"Jesse might not be happy about but he's alive making that good news" they all nodded in agreement. Dorie looked at Doctor.

"Do you think you could have someone, update us on Maddie ?"

"Of course. Also, I will be here, for a few more hours, and you can have me paged."

JoJo came back out.

"Um… so Maddie was dehydrated, bad. She is still on fluids, she's doing a lot better considering her condition. "

Paul looked at JoJo, concerned.

"Joelle, you don't sound excited about her doing better."

"Oh Mr. Wiseman"

"Paul"

"Oh Paul, I'm just regretting, how I spoke with you all, earlier.

Deacon, he's a good boy. He got caught up in some bad kids. Deac lives with me, now, I'm trying to set him straight."

Dori came around and hugged Joelle.." Kids are not easy, just ask my dad, right now mine are probably terrorizing their nana."

Joelle looked at Paul.

"Lynne?" Paul nodded "oh they are not terrorizing Lynne, maybe Lynne is terrorizing them.

They all laughed.

"Anyway, I would let Maddie rest, and unfortunately Jesse is still out of it, with the drugs he's on.." Joelle let that sentence drift off. "Maybe, you all should head home and get some rest, I'm on til 7 am, so I'll call you, if anything changes."

The Wisemans looked at each other and nodded, they were exhausted, nothing to do here.

They said goodbye to Jojo and left.

On the way out, Benny ran right into Doctor Waylon. "Oh my Gosh, Doctor Waylon, I'm so sorry." So wasn't Sis, the name her family and friends called Shirley Waylon, running into Benny was like running into a brick wall, he was solid muscle.

"It's okay, I'm fine."

Both Paul and Dorie chuckled

"Doctor, I bet running into Benny was like running into a brick wall." Sis laughed and nodded.

"I really am sorry," Benny said.

Touching Sis' shoulder, Sis looked up, at first she thought she was in pain, then realized it was like Benny gave her a shock. She looked at him, and realized Benny felt it.

"Okay, well I have a patient, see you tomorrow."

Sis rushed off.

"Let's go Daddy is starving."

Chapter 3

Tyler couldn't believe his luck lately, a great job that he loved.

A beautiful girlfriend, that he loved too and an adorable puppy. What more could he want?

"Juneau?"

"Frankie? What's the matter?"

"Tyler, hypothetically, if I was short a wrestler at a house show, could you fill in? It's not the WWE, but it's good fun and a charitable event."

"Hypothetically?"

"Yeah. Suppose I asked you a question like that, you know a favor. It would be a big draw. Tyler Juneau."

Tyler wanted to jump up and down, someone was asking him to wrestle, entertainment wrestling. It took him his composure to tell Frankie, he had to get a clear from his doctor.

"Hurry up Juneau, I need an answer like yesterday."

Tyler called his doctor and therapist. They both cleared him. Tyler called Andy, excited as hell. After he told Andy his news, Andy told Tyler about Jesse.

"Oh my God, did they catch him?"

Andy told Tyler about how Lynne

killed the shooter. Tyler blew out a breath.

"Remind me never to mess Lynne."

"Yeah, Tyler, get us some tickets, I know I'll be there, I'm sure Anna and Vee, I can ask the others, might do them good to get out of the house."

"I will, I didn't tell Anna, yet.

"Got it, when is it?"

"The weekend, bring the kids, it's a charity event, I guess there will be carnival games."

"Okay."

Tyler and Andy hung up. Now to tell Anna.

As Tyler and Anna's relationship progressed, she now found herself over Tyler's more often than not, today she picked up Chinese takeout, and headed over to Tyler's place. Anna was really proud of Tyler, he was a hard worker, and his handicap never put him down. Anna went into the kitchen, Tyler was cooking,

Anna held up the bag.

"Chinese"

"Homemade chicken fingers "

Anna slid her hand around his waist, kissing his back.

"wow! Those look great."

Tyler turned to face her. Gosh, did he love her?

"Babe, I gotta tell you something, and I don't want you to get upset."

"What? Are you okay?"

"I'm okay, Anna."

He held her close, he wasn't sure how she would react.

"Frankie called, and offered me a job"

"I thought you already had a job, with Frankie, training"

"Yeah, this is a little different."

"Is it legal?"

"Anna."

Tyler made Anna sit down.

"Tyler spit it out."

"There is a charity event the weekend and Frankie is short a wrestler, he asked me to fill in."

"Fill in what?"

"A match, wrestle"

"Tyler." her voice lowered,

"Baby, it's not what you think. I'm not going to get hurt. I know, it's a lot to take in. Just don't get upset."

"No, I'm not upset. I am worried. What if you move on from me someday."

"Move on, Anna?" Tyler looked both hurt and confused.

"You're Tyler Juneau."

"Yeah."

"Tyler, if you go on to the WWE,

you are not going to want to stay here in little Poland, Maine."

"It's not the WWE, and nobody said I'm moving anywhere, it's one night Anna, one night someone didn't show up, Frankie needs a body. We are a long way from WWE, come on.

Look, forget it, if you don't want me to do it, I'm out. I don't want to lose you, over this."

"Tyler, just do it, you were all lit up like a Christmas tree, telling me. I'm not going to take that away from you."

"Baby, are you sure? I'm not kidding, you mean more to me than some match."

"Tell Frankie you're in."

Tyler called Frankie.

"Hey Frankie, yeah we're good."Tyler's eyes went up to Anna. "Yeah, she's okay, why? Alright. Bye"

Anna knew the next question.

"Why did Frankie want to know if you were ok?"

"I have no idea."

Anna tried to look everywhere but at Tyler.

"Anna."

"It's okay, I'll ask Suzette if she wants me to work the weekend, "

"Aren't you coming with me."

"No, I don't think so."

"Why not?"

"I'm just not in the mood for guys banging into each other"

"What?"

"I just don't want to go, ok."

The hurt was written all over Tyler's face. Anna backpedaled, she didn't want to hurt him. She loved Tyler, but love wouldn't stop him from leaving, it wouldn't stop him from looking at the girls in the stands that, give them the opportunity, will bed any athlete.

"Okay, I'll come, you think it's okay to bring Sadie?"

Hearing her name, Sadie wagged her tail.

"Well, hey maybe, if he wants Tyler Juneau, he's gotta accept Anna and Tyler's baby Sadie Juneau."

"Goof."

"Goof GOOF is that the best you got? Comon Shaw Comon. Show me, what you got."

Tyler grabbed Anna, by the waist, and half dragged her to the couch, she was laughing hysterically.

"Goofy Juneau."

Tyler pretended to cover Anna for the pin, but she put a knee up and he fell on the floor. Anna jumped on him and whacked the floor three times.

Standing up fast, Anna adjusted her clothes.

"That will teach you, to mess with Shaw girls."

They were both laughing like crazy.

"I love you, Anna"

"I love you more, Goofy."

More laughter.

Chapter 4

Noah, was anxious. It was Saturday and he wanted to go ride his horse. His problem was Noah knew that once the adults got done with breakfast and chores, they would go see their Uncle Jesse.

Noah loved his uncle, he idolized Jesse and told everyone who listened that one day he would be Sheriff in Poland. Jesse believed him, Noah was little, the baby of the Wiseman clan, but the kid was a quick learner. Jesse actually got a hoot when mimicked him , when Jesse cleaned his gun, Noah cleaned his toy gun. When Noah found out Jesse was shot, he cried for two days. Plus, Aunt Maddie was sick, Mom would be taking care of her for a few days, and Max would pick up Mom's chores.

Nobody was around to take me riding, Noah thought to himself, but I need to see Braydon.

Braydon was Noah's prizewinning pony, the colt was the mating of two Champion show horses. Max actually owned the colt and parents, but let only the kids ride them.

Noah, told Nana Lynne, that he was going to check on Moose and Tiny. Noah knew he was fibbing but he had to see Braydon, he headed towards the stables. Halfway there, Noah felt someone watching him, he was only six, but he had sharp senses that karate taught him.

A little ways more, Noah knew he wasn't alone, four boys had him surrounded.

"Hey shrimp, how's your uncle, is he dead, yet."

Noah tried to keep walking, but the boys closed in on him. Trying to push through them , one of them struck Noah. Going down , Noah took out his whittle knife, Uncle Jesse said, if anything happens to them, to leave something behind. Noah placed the knife, in the grass, just before he was struck in the head.

Lynne went outside to tell Noah to come in and have a snack.

She knew Noah was upset about not being able to go see his colt.

"Noah! Come on, I have some of your favorite cookies."

No answer. For some weird reason, Lynne got a chill down her back.

"Noah? "

Lynne went back into the house.

"Noah?" Lynne started to panic. She went to the phone.

"Hi Max, is Noah with you?"

"Hey Lynne, no is he supposed to be?"

"He's gone missing, he told me, he was going to check on Moose. He wasn't there, I thought maybe he snuck down there."

"Lynne, I'm gonna come up, I'm going to walk up the trail, that the older kids take to school."

"Okay."

"Lynne, we'll find him. Probably got tired and sat down for a while."

Lynne went to the parlor, sat down on the couch and cried. She cried and prayed. Please don't let anything happen to that little boy, Lord. Bring that child home.

Moose and Tiny came into the home, through their doggie door, they curled up with Lynne.

Max came up the trail, keeping his eyes open for Noah. The little boy was obsessed with horses, the trail was far. Noah may have sat down under a tree and fallen asleep. Max got a little way up the trail, he spotted something glittering in the sun, shiny. Bending to pick it up, Max knew what it was before he reached for it. It was Noah's whittle knife, that Paul gave him for his 6 th birthday. Max also found signs of struggle, a smart kid. Walking to the Wiseman's home, Max thought how anyone could hurt a kid. He got to the house, Lynne looked so hopeful, but Max showed her the knife and Lynne broke down. Max caught her in his arms.

"Lynne we need to be strong, call Doug, we need him to start looking, tell him, it deals with what happened to Jesse. Those kids have Noah. I'm calling Dorie. She and Paul will need to come home.

Chapter 5

Andy was in the middle of a really intense workout when his phone rang. It was Paul, Jesse's dad. Andy knew both Jesse and Maddie were in the hospital. Andy and Vee intended to visit, but now Lynne and Max needed help searching for Noah.

Andy called Tyler.

"Andy we will be there in a few minutes.

Tyler told Anna, what was going on, over at the Wiseman's.

"I'll be ready, in a minute Tyler, call Suzette and tell her what's going on, I know she'll want to help.

Suzette's husband Steve trains search and rescue dogs, which would be a big help.

Tyler and Anna got to the Wiseman's ranch. Dorie was hyperventilating, Max was trying to calm her down. Andy and Vee pulled up and made all the introductions. Andy wished Maddie was here, she was still in the hospital, they were watching the baby, but nobody really knew why, Maddie was a super sleuth.

Praying for his two friends to be okay, Andy went over to Tyler.

"Hey Buddy, how are you doing."

"Andy, I actually feel guilty because life is so good for me right now."

"No man, don't feel guilty, we will find Noah. Maddie and Jesse will be fine."

"I met the Sherif, once. Solid guy."

"Yeah, Tyler, he is."

Paul gathered everyone together for a prayer.

"Okay, the trail goes from our house to the stables. What we are looking for are signs of struggle or anything you might think a six-year-old boy would have in his pocket. Noah, is young, but he's smart, he could have dropped anything. Marbles, he played

with marbles and jacks, always had them in his pockets."

Off to the side, Suzette's husband Steve had the dogs out, he was letting them sniff some of Noah's stuff.

Dorie's other kids, Scott and Katie were with their mother and

Max. The kids tried to control their crying, because they wanted to go on the trip.

People came from the Maine police, sheriff's office, school and hospital, Dr. Roman, Dr. Waylon other concerned parents. So many people that they were able to set up lots of lines.

Benny spotted Dr. Waylon, she looked alone. Shirley Waylon was a beautiful woman, she could have been a model.

Benny took a deep breath

"Hi Dr. Waylon"

Shirley turned and looked at Benny, he had a sheepish look on his face.

"Oh hi. Benny, right? How's Jesse? I've been off since yesterday, I came by to help."

"Jesse is the same, still not responding. They kept Maddie too, they are concerned about the baby."

"I'm so sorry about that, sometimes in Jesse's case the loss of blood, it takes time."

"Yeah, that's what King told us. So you here with your boyfriend or husband."

Way to be subtle Ben.

"No husband no boyfriend, just here with friends trying to find Noah. "

"I can't believe, he walked away from the house like that.. my parents would have killed us. You met my father, right?"

Shirley laughed. Benny was cute and funny. Rumor at the hospital was that he is gay though, 'Of course,' Shirley said to herself.

"I better get back to my friends they will be starting a search soon."

"Yeah me too, my family probably waiting on me."

"See ya, Benny"

"Bye Doctor Waylon. "

"Sis."

"I'm sorry?" Benny looked confused.

"My name it's Shirley, but my friends and family call me Sis"

"Ooooh okay."

They looked at each other for a long moment.

"BENNY." Paul's voice echoed through the crowd.

Benny laughed, gave a little wave, started to walk away then turned around.

"Hey Sis." Sis turned. "Would you like to go out to dinner sometime?" Benny held his breath.

"Yeah, of course, I was under the impression.. "

She let her sentence hang.

"Oh." Benny deflated a little.

Being left speechless, he just nodded and walked away.

Of course, she knew he was gay, that's you Benny, Benny the homosexual. Nobody ever thought a person could like both sexes, unheard of. Walking towards his family, Benny exhaled and out loud, he cursed.

"Fuck"

Paul looked up from the huddle the Wisemans formed. Walking over to his son.

"Look, Ben, I know you've been through a lot, but this is no place to air your frustrations, you hear me? Get it together."

Benny nodded, taking a deep breath, Benny faced his family.

"Sorry."

Dorie was inconsolable, tears flowing. Max tried holding her, but she pushed him off of her. He knew she was not being herself but he wanted to be there for her.

Andy, Vee, Tyler, Anna, Suzette, and Steve made up another group. Other groups are made up of friends and family.

Joey, Nola, Jimmy, and Jackie close friends of Maddie's wanted to help. Edna set up a refreshment table and of course the folks from the hospital.

Everyone was here to see Noah home safe.

The sheriff's department came over to the Wiseman's.

"Everyone ready, let's go find Noah. "

Max grabbed Dorie's hand when she went to pull back, he held it tight.

"No"

Dorie relaxed her grip, and looked at Max "Max."

"Babe, you know how I feel about you and the kids, Don't push me away, having Noah out there, know sure and well, he was heading to the stables. Don't push me out, Dorie please."

Dorie pulled Max close, pulling him down to kiss his mouth. "Come on , let's go find our little boy."

Chapter 6

Noah knew he was in trouble, those big kids put a sack over his head and put him in a car. He overheard them talking about a cottage in the woods. All Noah wanted to do was see Braydon.

'My mother will punish me for sure,' his six-year-old brain, thinking more of his mother, than the torment that these boys put him through. Once he was in the sack, they kicked at him, a couple landing against his head. Noah cried, the pain, his head was bleeding, he wanted his mother. The boys left him alone, Noah cried out, but his voice was a tiny sound in an empty forest. "I'm hungry, Mommy please come find me, I'm cold and hungry."

At the hospital, Joelle was covering one of the nurses who went on the search. Putting her mind, on auto-pilot, Joelle thought about the missing little boy. She looked up to see Deacon run into the intern's locker room, his clothes dirty like mud. He ran into the locker room, with his eyes like a deer caught in headlights. Joelle through up a quick prayer. Lord,

don't let that boy have had anything to do with that little boy's disappearance. The searchers out for hours now, with no sign of

Noah. Joelle regretted being wrong but needed reassurance that Deacon could not have been involved. Joelle followed Deacon around and watched him like a hawk with a bunny.

A few times Deacon caught Joelle watching him, he was sure it was his imagination but he thought he saw a scowl, on Joelle's face. He was so busy, trying to read his aunt's facial expression that he ran right into Dr Roman. Dr Roman fell and Deacon fell on top of him, landing on King's privates. King let out a howl, that matched Jesse's from the other day.

Joelle was down the hall and on top of Deacon, in a heartbeat. Grabbing him up by his scrubs, Joelle picked up Deacon, off of Dr. Roman.

"What on earth are you doing

Deacon, you hurt Dr. Roman."

"I'm sorry, I got distracted."

"Distracted, get your head out of your butt. Go home."

"Joelle, that's not necessary, I'm okay, I'm sure it was an accident." King winced in pain and looked at Deacon.

"Yeah, I'm sorry Dr. Roman."

"Dr. Roman, he needs to be punished he's been acting up, a lot lately. I really don't need him in trouble with the sheriff's dept again."

"I know Joelle, but sending him home isn't really punishment, working in the kitchen, that's punishment."

"You could be on to something there. Go on back to work Deacon, I'll deal with you later."

Deacon flew out of there.

"I'm really sorry Dr. Roman."

"King, call me King, ahh he's still a kid."

"Yeah, but at the same age, his father started messing up. His dad is in jail, and he and some other kids decide to haunt the Sheriff. "

King looked in the direction of Jesse's room.

"Haunt?"

"According to Deacon, he wasn't there, when the Sheriff got shot. Dorie Wiseman said Deacon threatened the Sheriff.

I don't know Dr. Roman.

"King. "King smiled at Joelle.

"I guess it's something that bares watching, Joelle. I've known Dorie, awhile, never known her to lie."

Noah could feel the cold night.

Mommy, where are you, please come find me. The darkness, consumed Noah. He started to cry.

"Please come find me, Mommy"

Chapter 6

The Sheriff's Department search was called off due to nightfall.

A lot of people, stayed with lanterns guiding them in their search for Noah. Dorie was being watched closely by Max, he saw a lot of signs, that she was going to snap. People stopped by to ask if she was ok.

Max was like, she's doing ok, but saying to himself. Are people really asking her that question?

Max leaned down and told Dorie maybe she should go lie down. She slapped him.

"Are you stupid? Do you really think that my son is out there cold, hungry, crying?"

Max tried to hold her. Dorie pushed him off.

"Leave, leave, just get out, I don't need such foolishness, in my life. Go lay down."

Max stood turning toward the door. Paul walked toward him.

"Max, don't leave, go in the kitchen, let her calm down. Dorie doesn't mean what she said."

Steve Lin, Paul's best friend blocked Max's way. He said, "Max."

"She's lashing out, she had to pick you, because she knew you would understand. Dorie knows

you won't leave her. She just wants her little boy."

Max really tried to hold it in, he was trying really had to be strong. The only problem was the picture in his head of Noah, the first time he rode Braydon, the kid was a natural.

"I need some fresh air."

Andy came up behind Max and put an arm around his shoulders.

"Sounds like a great idea, Let's go breathe in the Maine air. Nothing beats Maine in November." Two weeks from

Thanksgiving, the cool and crisp, leaves underfoot. Max

left Steve and led him outside.

Vee, Anna, Suzette, and Lynne circled around Dorie. Suzette's husband Steve and other dog handlers were prepared to work through the night. Dorie's eyes were almost swollen shut with tears, but she had to talk to Max.

"I have to talk to Max."

Tyler, who had been just off to the side, chimed in.

"Give him a little time, Dorie.

Guys have feeling too, I saw how hurt Max was"

"That's why I want to talk to him, who exactly are you again?"

Anna realizing Tyler was in trouble, went to say something but Tyler brushed her off.

"I'm Anna's boyfriend Tyler."

Making no attempt to shake Dorie's hand, in fear of losing his.

"Guys are different, we process differently. Give him time and space, he will come back to you."

Dorie looked at Vee. Vee nodded. Dorie sighed and leaned back, she reached out to Tyler.

"It's nice to meet you, Tyler.

Tyler, smiled and shook Dori's hand. He then pulled Anna off to the side.

"I'm going to take the car and drive a little way up. There are some abandoned cottages, I want to check. Older kids are always hanging around up there, boys bring their dates up there for some hanky panky, if you get my drift."

"Hanky panky?"

Tyler blushed. "You know what I mean."

"You want me to come with you?"

"No, You stay here."

"Okay, just be careful. Love you."

"Yeah, I will. Love you more."

Tyler got outside and told Andy and Max he'd be back. It was better, if he went alone, he knew how to talk to anyone, he ran into.

Vee looked at Anna, something was up. Grabbing her sister's hand, she whispered in her ear.

"Where did Tyler really go?"

Anna fidgeted.

"Anna?" Vee snapped.

"The old abandoned cabins up north"

"Is he crazy, you know there's people up there that could really hurt. "

"No, He said that they were abandoned."

Vee headed for the door.

Andy turned as Vee ran over to him and Max. "Babe?"

"Tyler went to the old abandoned cabins up north."

"Alone?" Vee nodded.

"Get Paul and Benny. Why didn't he mention it to the cops?"

Andy got the sheriff dept on the phone and told Doug where they were heading. Doug was furious.

"In the middle of the freaking night, Andy. I have all my best home resting for tomorrow's search."

"I know Doug, I'd have gone myself but.." Andy let the sentence hang.

"You're not the law, Andy. I can't understand why people try to do dangerous things on their own.

I just sent out the only two cars I have. Thanks for the heads-up, it is a good lead. "

Paul and Steve came out on the porch. Paul looked at Andy.

"I'm sorry pal, you're staying here."Andy nodded. Max said to Paul.

"I'm coming."

"Fine, but you keep your emotions in check." Max nodded. Paul looked around.

"Where's Benny?"

No one knew, they couldn't wait, so Paul, Steve, and Max got in Paul's truck and headed North.

Chapter 7

The temperature dropped.

Noah was cold, he tried again to get out of the sack but it was latched at the top with a metal clasp. Noah started crying again.

Noah heard the door open, scuffling across the floor. Trying, to be quiet, Noah stopped crying. He had a gut feeling that these people weren't for him, there was a girl and she was giggling. Noah heard clothes falling on the floor, heavy breathing, gasping, the girl letting out a small cry. Then nothing, a few minutes later, clothes rustling, then the door opened. Noah called out The girl turned.

"What was that?" she asked.

"Nothing, let's go."

Noah cried for help, next he heard something thud to the floor. The boy had knocked the girl out. Noah felt a hard kick in his ribs.

"Stupid, now I have to get rid of both of you." The boy said and left.

Tyler knows he should be afraid, he remembered stumbling across these cabins years ago.

They were abandoned by people mostly kids used them.

Tyler checked the first two cabins and turned up nothing. In the third cabin, he found a man in there, he was most likely a squatter. Tyler went to turn away, he could see Noah wasn't in there. Tyler turned straight into the barrel of a shotgun. A huge man, built like a mountain.

"What's your business."

"Please, I'm lost" Tyler held up his hands. "I mean no harm."

"Give me your money and that watch and the gold chain."

Benny crept up so slowly on Mountain Man. Even Tyler didn't know where he came from.

"Lower that firearm. This is the police."

Shockingly, he did. Benny breathed a sigh of relief.

"Alright, we are sorry we disturbed you guys, we are looking for a little boy. We have reason to believe, he was taken."

Mountain man, whose name was Joel.

"All kinds of kids up here use the cabin for lovers lane. The 6th or 7th one is like a revolving door no tell motel. The one on the end, older boys use as a clubhouse." Benny's eyes lit up.

"Bingo."

Benny thanked Joel and slipped him a couple of hundred bucks, to Tyler he said.

"Come on, Inspector, let's see if we can find Noah."

Back at the house, Dorie started getting restless.

"Why did they stop looking? They wouldn't be stopped if it were the mayor's kid, would they?"

Everyone agreed with her.

"Anyone see my father and Benny?"

Vee just stayed quiet. Dorie went on.

"What about Max? Did he leave?"

"I don't think so, I thought I saw them on the porch earlier," Vee said.

Dorie turned and headed for the door. Stepping out on the porch, Dorie hadn't found Max, which kind of upset her.

"That's weird. Where are they?"

Suzette's husband Steve led the handlers, and they stumbled upon the cabins. The direction they had come in from was the back of what looked like an old abandoned campground. Right then, Steve's dog Cody sounded off with a howl. Next, his brother

Randy's dog Riley sounded off.

Noah was here or had been here.

Benny turned in the direction of the dogs and took off running,

Tyler was behind him but just at a slower pace. Benny got to Steve and showed him his credentials.

"How do you want to do this?"

"If there is anyone in there, besides Noah, they might do something stupid if they get spooked. They no doubt heard the dogs."

Steve nodded. Benny said.

"I'm going to go around the back of this cottage. Have your team ready. "

The sheriff's dept showed up. Benny cursed silently, if anyone was inside they no doubt heard the sirens.

No one came out, no movement inside. Benny went to the door and went to knock. Maine police showed up. Once again, Benny cursed under his breath.

The police rushed to the door, knocking the door right off the hinges with one kick.

Empty the cabinet was empty.

Noah heard the commotion outside, he started yelling trying not to lose his little voice.

"Help me!" His voice was so tiny.

The girl woke to Noah's cries.

She screamed.

"Help."

Benny heard her.

"Over here."

It was hard to see in the dark forest.

Another car pulled up, it was Paul, Steve, and Max. They stayed back, and let them bust the door in. The police went to kick the door in, but it swung open.

In the middle of the floor, was a little sack.

"Benny?" one of the officers said. The girl let out a huge wail.

The officers raised their weapons but it was another sack. Everyone poured into the room as they got Benny and the girl out of the sacks.

"Uncle Benny! Grandpa."

Noah ran to them.

The call went in that Noah was found.

Chapter 8

"Mama" Jesse's voice was groggy. Joelle picked up her head, she's been sitting with Jesse, in Maddie's absence. She

didn't understand it, but just felt the right thing to do.

"Jesse?"

"Mama, I can't go to school today, I'm not feeling so good."

Joelle smiled, he must have been a cute kid. She rang the buzzer for the nurse. Yes, she was a nurse, but off duty.

The floor nurse came running in.

"Joelle?"

"Your patient is awake. Asked for his Mama, said he wasn't well enough to go to school today. "

"He is a cutie, his wife is down the hall, baby on board."

"Fiancée, not married yet."

"You try to talk to him?"

Joelle shook her head no, she was just a body standing in for family, while they searched for their little boy.

"Any word on his nephew?"

Pat looked shocked Joelle didn't know.

"They found him! Old abandoned cabins up North. Bunch of punk kids, caught one, his girlfriend gave him up. They think he was going to come back and kill them both."

"What?"

"He knocked the girl out, she was barely conscious when the cops got there."

"But how do they know, he was planning on killing them."

"The girl told the cops, that the sack was just something, he needed to take care of. The little boy heard, now I have both of you to get rid of"

"Oh my Goodness, do they know who, it could be?"

"Not really, but they do know the bunch of kids who hang there. They are trying to locate the owner of the cabin."

Joelle looked at her cell phone.

She ignored a bunch of calls, but there it was. Maine Police, Jo shook her head, "Oh, Deacon."

The doctor came into the room, but it wasn't Doctor Roman. Jesse didn't respond again.

"I guess we give him time." the Doctor said.

The two nurses nodded. Pat and Doctor left Joelle alone with Jesse. Jo just put her head in her hands, then started praying for Jesse and Maddie again.

Noah had to be taken to the hospital, all he wanted to do was see his mom. Grandpa told him, his mom was on the way to the hospital to meet Noah. The tears would not stop flowing from Paul's eyes, it wasn't just Noah, but the last week was horrible. All that started, cause kids wanted to avenge their parents, the law was wrong, and their parents did no wrong.

Grand Larceny, Attempted murder, Hit Run, and Distribution of illegal narcotics, Jesse told Paul every one of these crimes. Now, their kids were going to be in the system, how screwed up was that. Most people hope their kids come home from school or a night out with friends. If your kid is in public service a firefighter, cop, paramedic, or in the service, they make it home safe. These punks came to hurt my son, then my grandson. I'm going to make sure each and every one of them in that gang is prosecuted to the very limits of the law.

Dorie was at the emergency room entrance, five ambulances came in not Noah. Dorie put her head in her hands, and another ambulance, they were unloading the stretcher. Dorie gasped.

"Noah!"

"Mommy!"

the medics asked Dorie to please move back, they needed to the little boy into the hospital.

"Sorry" Dorie said.

"Dorie."

Dorie turned. "Lisa." it was Steve Lin's girlfriend.

"Dorie, I heard, I hope Noah is okay."

"Thank you."

Everyone else went back to the house, Lynne was 8 1/2 months pregnant. She was really supposed to be on bed rest, not babysitting.

Paul called her.

"How is my baby Mama?"

"You are never allowed to touch me again."

"lol You okay, babe?"

"I'm fine Paul, how is everyone."

"Noah is good. Shift change, so I'm going to see how Jesse and Maddie are doing."

"Okay keep me posted.

Paul hung up. He got to Jesse's room.

"Joelle?" Paul was confused.

"Hi. I hope it was ok. I didn't want him to wake up to nobody here."

"Joelle, thank you. That was really nice of you. Jo, the problem is. I think maybe, Deacon was involved in this kidnapping and assault. I'm sorry to tell you that because you are a really good person."

Joelle nodded, she had been trying to get Deacon on the phone, no answer. He hasn't shown up for his shift either. Joelle didn't know what to think or believe.

"Paul, I hope you're are wrong.

Deacon keeps telling me he's not involved. That he was there at your house but didn't do anything."

"Knowingly, witnessing a crime and not reporting it, is kind of a crime. You know that Joelle."

Joelle nodded again. How could she defend Deacon when her head was telling her otherwise?

Dr Roman came to the door, of Jesse's room. Greeting Paul and Joelle, he went to Jesse's bedside.

"I heard Jess, was alert."

Joelle, who had taken what Paul said personally, said, "Dr Roman, I was here, he was calling out for his mom."

Paul sighed.

King looked from Joelle to Paul.

"Is something going on?"

"No, son everything is fine. It's just me, thinking of Jesse's mom."

King looked at Joelle.

"I'm fine Dr. Roman, I was just sitting with Jesse, his wife is still being watched."

"I was just with her, she is ready to be discharged, Paul."

"Knowing Maddie, she is going to straight to this room."

"You got that right, Dad."

Maddie wobbly walked to the chair next to Joelle. King laughed and shook his head.

"You need to go home and get in bed for a while Maddie, think of the baby.

Jesse groaned out the name.

"Maddie." his throat felt like sandpaper.

Maddie flew to the bedside.

"Jesse!!"

Jesse let out a huge sigh.

King went over to the other side

"Hey brother, let's check some stuff. "Jesse did really well, squeezing fingers, following fingers.

"I'm going to say five words say them back to me, backwards. Roman King you love I"

Without thinking Jesse said back the words"

"I love you King Roman."

"Awww Jesse, I love you too."

Then they all try to tell Jesse

what has been going on."

"Sweet Jesus. I'm tired now."

King said to the others.

"You guys should give him some rest, now. I noticed Jesse's eyes still looked glazed, hopefully, bed rest will, you too Maddie"

"I'm not going to harm yourself or that baby."

Jesse sat up "Baby ?" his eyes flew to Maddie. "Mads?"

Maddie gave a little smile and nodded.

Chapter 9

Tyler was back to the Wiseman farm to pick up Anna. It had been a very emotional night, where things could have gone very wrong. Tyler knocked at the door, Lynne opened it.

Tyler greeted Lynne, she smiled back, Tyler knew he was in for a lecture.

"I'm sorry Lynne, I should have known better."

"It's okay, Tyler. I'm sure you were trying to do the right thing."

Tyler and Lynne had met, when Tyler first moved to Maine, he had a bit of a stalker situation.

The girl had wanted to take care of Tyler, after his amputations, which Tyler thought was sweet.

He told the girl, he wasn't up to people or a relationship, at that time. The girl would not give up and Tyler called the Sheriff's office. Lynne showed up. She talked to the girl and finally, the girl decided to leave. Tyler remembered asking Lynne, what she said to the girl. Lynne opened her notebook and read back. Yes, ma'am, that's what I was told, it doesn't work.

Tyler asking Lynne, what didn't work. Lynne looked down at Tyler's private. Tyler and Lynne had been friends ever since.

"Anna is in the kitchen"

"Okay."

Tyler went into the kitchen, Anna was packing up food in Tupperware.

"Hey."

Anna spun around and faced Tyler. A sigh of relief came out of her.

"Are you okay? Are you hungry?"

"I'm okay Anna, I didn't even do anything. All the law enforcement showed up, just as I got there. Benny probably saved my life."

Anna looked at Tyler. "What?"

"Yeah, trust me, I won't try being a superhero, ever again,"

Tyler told Anna, what happened

with the mountain men, and how Benny probably showed up at the right time.

"I really owe Benny," Tyler said.

Noah was scared, but loving the attention. The Doctors finally let

Dorie in the room. Noah started rushing her about Jesse, Aunt Maddie, Nana Lynne, Scotty, Katy, Moose, and Tiny.

"Mommy, has anyone checked on Braydon?"

Dorie threw her eyes to heaven.

Lord, this child of mine.

"I'm sure Braydon is fine, Noah.

How are you feeling, baby."

"I'm okay, where's Mr Max?"

Thinking to herself, I wish I knew.

"I'm not sure, Noah, maybe he went to check on Bray."

That made sense to Noah. Dorie had tried Max's cell phone earlier, when she left for the hospital. Straight to voicemail. That had upset Dorie, where was Max, it really was unlike him. He was usually, there when she needed him, always her strong shoulder now. Surely, Max knew Dorie was only acting out because of what happened to Noah. She hadn't meant anything she said.

Especially not to him.

Paul came into the room, followed by what looked like a yellow beach ball. Lynne was 8 1/2 months pregnant and showed it.

"Noah, what happened?"

Paul said kissing Dorie, on the top of her head. Dorie leaned into Paul's body as he put his arm around her. Lynne sat down, wishing this baby would just come out already.

"I wanted to check on Braydon,

Grandpa."

"Noah, you know Max takes great care of all the horses."

Scotty and Katie nodded. They wanted to know just how much trouble Noah was in.

"Miss Tammy takes care of Bray,

Grandpa, but.."

"Come on Noah, you wanted to ride Braydon, and no one was going to stop you. Do you know how bad this could have turned out?"

Noah started to cry. Paul didn't want to reprimand Noah, in the hospital room, but if you let it go, he wouldn't learn, from this almost deadly mistake.

Dorie followed Paul's way of parenting so there was no 'Come on, Dad, he's just a kid.'

She had actually thought about punishing Noah, when he got out of the hospital, but her three kids hanging on to their grandfather's every word. Dorie would probably call that punishment enough.

"Do you guys understand Grandpa?" Dorie said to her kids. "We love you guys so much, if anything ever happened to you, we would be so sad."

Noah sat straight up and hugged his mother, squeezing her like only Noah did.

"I'm sorry Mommy."

"I know baby, it doesn't make it any less scary, you saw what they did to Uncle Jesse. Noah, there are bad people out there, okay."

Dorie looked at her munchkins, reliving that moment when she heard Noah was missing. The three kids were nodding, when the doctor came into the room.

"I'm looking for Noah Wiseman."

Noah raised his hand like he was in more trouble.

Well, Noah, how would you like to get out of this place? Do you want to go home with your brother and sister?

Noah jumped out of bed.

Everyone laughed.

"Well, you may want to put some pants on, there's a couple of nurses out there with a crush on you."

"Yessir."

Noah flew to his closet, his bare bottom, flashing everyone. Dorie couldn't have loved her kids more, when Katie and Scotty tried to block everyone's view.

Chapter 10

Max fiddled around the stables, for what seemed to be hours. Looking up at the time, Max thought, '45 minutes, that's not possible.' He checked his watch.

46 minutes.

Max missed Dorie and the kids. He missed Jesse, I'm not going to cry he thought to himself. There was a loud bang like one of the stable doors blew open.

"Mr. Max!" Oh, Thank Goodness. Max, threw up a silent prayer.

Turning to see, the kids and Dorie, those tears did form. Noah ran to Max, throwing his arms around his legs.

"I'm sorry, Mr Max."

Max picked up Noah, crushing him to his chest, Noah is not Max's biological son, but the love Max had for these three kids.

"Noah! You scared the crap out of me. I love you, Scotty and Katie, so much. Please don't ever do something like that again." Now all three kids were crying, clinging to Max.

"Go on, go check on the horses."

The kids dropped their hugs and ran to the horses.

'Guess I don't compete with horses,' Max said to himself.

Dorie watched Max, she saw 50 shades of pride run over his face. He wasn't going to be the one to crack, his eyes focused on the ground. No other woman ever made Max feel the way Dorie did, then again no other woman ever made him feel. At one point in his life, Max thought he was dead inside, he never felt love. Until Dorie. Dorie brought Max back to life, she made him feel, her touch electrified him, her look melted him, her kisses stunned him and their lovemaking stole his breath. Even now thoughts of their rhythm made Max breathless.

Max wasn't mad at Dorie, he was hurt when she lashed out at him, and it cut him to his core.

"Hey." Dorie's voice was tiny.

Max looked up. Dorie sighed.

"Max, I'm sorry, I shouldn't have lashed out at you. I was just afraid, I never been so scared."

Max wanted to reach out and grab Dorie, but his heart hurt, he knew she had all the reasons in the whole to lash out. It still hurt.

"You know, Max, you are right, I can't begin to understand the hurt. Please find it in your heart to talk to me."

"What do you want to talk about?" Max kicked at the dirt.

Dorie looked up her eyes shiny with tears. Max folded like a cheap card table.

"Awww babe."

Max grabbed Dorie around the waist, kissing her hard, then pushing her against the stable wall, pressing his body against her so close, she felt his manhood, pushing into her. Dorie didn't want to, but backed him up a little, in case the kids came out. In a flustered voice she said "Later."

Noah followed by Scotty and Katie came running out.

"Mr Max, all the ponies look great."

"Well, I'm happy about that guys, I'm really glad you came to check on them."

Max's mind wasn't on horses, it was making love to Dorie, his mind was going crazy, his body even crazier. If the kids weren't here, he'd have thrown her down into a pile of hay. Dorie

moved as far as possible from Max, she saw the hunger in his

eyes. She was no better, imagining their lovemaking with her children right there.

"Mommy! "

Noah's lungs were definitely feeling better. Dorie looked at Noah.

"Noah, did the doctor, give you an extra set of lungs, at the hospital?"

Noah, made a very confused face.

"We are hungry, Mommy."

"Alright, let's get back to the house and see what Nana Lynne, cooked up."

Katie ran over to Max, grabbing his hand.

"Come on, Mr Max, time to eat."

"I'm coming Katie, but I have to tell Tammy, I'm leaving and close up."

Tammy came up, behind Max.

"Tammy can do that."

Max spun around. "Tammy!"

Dorie laughed.

"Tammy, you are welcome to join us. Lynne cooks for an army."

"I'd like to, but had riding lessons today, those kids killed me. Going to have a long soak and go to bed."

"Sounds good," Dorie said picturing herself and Max in the tub. She blushed, Max saw, and chuckled. Tammy saw the exchange.

"Wow, you two got it bad. Try to make it through supper." laughing Tammy gave a wave heading to the back of the stables.

Dorie headed for Paul's truck, hoping he didn't need it.

"Max, you riding with us?"

Max looked at Dorie, then at the kids, back at Dorie.

"It's about time they knew," Dorie said. "Are you okay with that?"

Max nodded. Okay? Max was thrilled. Dorie gathered the kids in a circle.

"Listen up, you guys, Mr Max and I want to let you know something." four pairs of eyes glued to Dorie, Max included.

"Mommy and Mr Max are boyfriend and girlfriend okay?"

The three kids laughed. Max and Dorie looked at each other.

"What's so funny?"

Scotty was the leader.

"We already know that Mommy."

"You do?"

Katie and Noah made kissy faces. Scott made googly eyes.

Dorie and Max started laughing, so hard.

"Okay, okay let's get my starving children home." She tossed the keys to Max.

They drove home.

Chapter 11

Saturday was here, Tyler was a nervous wreck, he wanted this match, then he didn't. He never wanted to back down from challenges, I'm Tyler Juneau. One of the things that bothered him most, getting embarrassed. Teaching students different techniques, was a whole lot easier than someone diving at you from top ropes.

Anna was more terrified than Max. The last thing she needed was him getting hurt, Ana saw a future with Tyler. Ana was in love with Tyler, and wanted to have a family with him. Anna knew that the lure of the ring was too tempting to Tyler. Anna was so proud of him, she swelled up with pride, when someone asked her a question about the charity match.

She loved Tyler, she knew he loved her too. Was it enough, there will be those groupies, always hanging around. Stop it, Ana. Tyler is not Craig. No, Tyler was so not like Craig. Craig was an egotistical narcissist, and everyone had seen that but Anna, she made excuses for him. The lying, the excuses, then Anna found out from the girl he was sleeping with. Craig was cheating on her, with some groupie following his band. The girl smelled of alcohol and her eyes were glassy, when confronted about what Anna was gonna do about the affair, Anna smiled at the girl and said, 'He's all yours." For some time, it did hurt a little, more like a pride thing, the hard part was it happened around the holidays. Suddenly, instead of enjoying being with family and friends, she stayed away to avoid questions and stares.

"Anna"

Anna shook her head. Andy, Vee,

Suzette and Steve were standing in front of her, Ana smiled "Hey guys! Let's go find a place, we can all sit together"

She started to walk toward the front rows, Anna's sisters caught up to her, and Vee said it first.

"He's not Craig, Anna."

"Hmmmmm?"

"We know you think every guy is going to turn into Craig."

"That's not true."

"So where was your head, just now."

"I'm worried about Tyler, that's it."

Anna gave her hair a twirl. Vee and Suzette looked at each other and smiled. Being triplets, they even had the same tell, their mom had told them about when they were twelve and they tried to squirm out punishment for going down the lake after dark.

"Sure you don't want to give that hair another twirl?"

Vee winked of Suzette.

"Okay, fine Tyler is the first guy,

I trusted since Craig. I can't go through that again."

Suzette just looked at Anna.

"Did he give you a reason to think that would happen?"

"No."

Just then, everyone started cheering, "Juneau, Juneau, Juneau."

Tyler made his way down the ramp, he waved to the crowd.

Suzette and Vee laughed.

"SPEEDOS!"

Anna laughed too.

Tyler continued down the ramp and walked over to Anna. What was most amazing his artificial limbs were so realistic that you could barely notice.

"Babe."

"Tyler?"

"I feel naked in this thong."

Vee and Suzette were whistling and doing cat calls. Andy and Steve pretended to be jealous.

Then it happened.

"Tyler." Tyler went from all smiles to all seriousness. Anna turned to the voice of the girl and then back to Tyler.

"Missy."

Melissa, his ex-girlfriend, of course, the one who broke his heart. Tyler was staring at her.

"Tyler?" Anna's voice cracked.

Tyler looked at Anna, like a lost boy.

"Juneau, quit stalling with the fans" Frankie yelled from across the ring.

Tyler looked at Missy, failing to realize Anna was watching his every move. Tyler went to look at Anna but it was too late, she was gone. Her sisters went to go after her, but Andy and Steve grabbed them. Andy said to them.

"Let her go, that had to hurt, but she needs to sort it out."

"Andy." Vee whined.

"Vee, Andy's right, she needs to be alone, right now."

Tyler wanted to go after Anna, he should have gone after Anna but he made a commitment. Turning to Vee and Suzette, Tyler pleaded with them.

"Please, get her to understand,

I love her and not the past."

Vee and Suzette nodded.

"Juneau."

Chapter 12

Back at the hospital, Maddie was walking around more, she was allowed to walk down to Jesse's room. Dragging her IV pole, Maggie slowly made it down to Jesse's room, pulled the chair over to his bed, slowly sat down, and put her head on his hand. Doctors were worried, Jesse hadn't woken up yet, and they were worried about brain damage, memory loss, and even death. The only encouragement was the fact that Jesse had woken up, and he even spoke.

Maddie began to cry, tears slowly running down her face, onto Jesse's hand.

"Dear Lord, bring him back to me. I need him, more than ever now, me and the baby need him."

Jesse stirred. Maddie's head snapped up.

"Mads?" Jesse felt like his mouth was full of cotton, his tongue made of sandpaper.

"Mads, don't cry, it only hit me in the shoulder, I'll be fine."

Maddie laughed, he didn't realize everything he'd been through in the last two weeks.

Jesse tried to sit up and the pain shot through his whole left side.

Maddie hit the buzzer. Joelle came into the room, saw Maddie then gasped when she saw Jesse's eyes open. Spinning around, Joelle went to get Doctor Roman.

"Doctor Roman."

"Joelle, slow down, you're going to fall or have an accident."

Joelle slid on some spilled water, right into Doctor Roman's arms.

"Well okay, this works for me"

King knew he was pushing his luck, Joelle could report him for harassment. Blushing, Jo straightened herself.

"Jesse's awake"

King smiled, he looked at Joelle, wanting her to read his eyes. Pleading with her, with his.

"Come on" Without thinking, Joelle grabbed King's hand.

Jo and King nearly collided with Paul and Lynne, who decided to check up on Maddie and Jesse.

Joelle couldn't contain her excitement. "Jesse is awake!"

It was almost comical how the four of them tried to get through the door at the same time.

Then they let Lynne in to sit.

King went over to Jesse.

"Hey Jess"

"Hey King, the shoulder is a little sore, might want to get an x-ray of it."

"Jesse, do you know you had surgery?"

"Come on, quit joking around."

"Jesse, I'm not joking. You had surgery, about a week ago. The bullet was lodged between bone and nerves, we had to go in and get it. It was a huge surgery and it was performed by Doctor Waylon.

"Sis?"

"Yeah, Sis, you remember her?"

"When I come here, she's here sometimes. She's nice."

To Maddie and Jo, King said.

"He's doing great other than not remembering the surgery, which is normal. Jesse, you are doing great."

"When can I go back to work? A month, six weeks?"

"Jess, let's talk about that later, we can run a few more tests."

"King, come on man, you look like deer caught in headlights. What are you hiding from me."

"Maddie." Joelle rushed over to Maddie and caught her before, she hit the floor.

"Mads." Jesse tried to get up and fell back in bed. "King, what's wrong with her. "he just noticed the IV pole. "Maddie?"

Maddie was just coming around.

"Mads?"

"I'm okay Jesse."

Jesse tried to contain his composure, but that was easy.

"Can someone tell me what the hell is going on here?"

Maddie let out a deep sigh.

"I'm pregnant, Jesse. Surprise."

Jesse, mouth hanging open, trying to find words."Pregnant?"

"Yeah, we are having a baby."

"King, sit me up."

"Jesse."

"King."

"Jesse, I can stand, I'll come to you, okay."

Poor Maddie, Jesse held her so tightly that he nearly crushed her ribs. As long as he's feeling better, Maddie thought to herself.

Paul and Lynne went over to help Maddie sit down. They did a little group hug.

www.ingramcontent.com/pod-product-compliance
Lightning Source LLC
Chambersburg PA
CBHW040842010826
48978CB00012BB/867